Pheasant and Kingfisher

Originally told by Nganalgindja in the Gunwinggu language

Written by Catherine Berndt   Illustrated by Arone Raymond Meeks

MONDO

First published in the United States of America in 1994 by
MONDO Publishing

First published in *Land of the Rainbow Snake* by Catherine Berndt, Collins, 1979.
Published in Australia in 1987 by Bookshelf Publishing Australia.

For information contact:
MONDO Publishing
980 Avenue of the Americas
New York, NY 10018

Printed in the United States of America
First MONDO Printing 1994
02 03 04   9 8 7 6 5

Original development by Snowball Educational

Photograph Credits Courtesy of Ashton Scholastic Pty Ltd: p. 1; Courtesy of the Berndt Museum/The University of Western Australia: p. 17.

Library of Congress Cataloging-in-Publication Data

Berndt, Catherine Helen.
     Pheasant and kingfisher : originally told by Nganalgindja in the Gunwinggu language / written by Catherine Berndt ; illustrated by Arone Raymond Meeks.
          p.   cm.
     Summary: Two men escape from danger by turning into birds in this Aboriginal myth from Australia which explains how the pheasant and kingfisher came into our world.
     ISBN 1-879531-70-4 : $21.95. — ISBN 1-879531-65-8: $9.95. —
ISBN 1-879531-64-X : $4.95
     [1. Australian aborigines—Folklore. 2. Birds—Folklore. 3. Folklore—Australia.] I. Meeks, Arone Raymond, ill. II. Title.
PZ8.1.B4168Ph 1994
398.2'099404528—dc20   94-29581
                                                                                              CIP
                                                                                              AC

My childhood memories are of my relatives in Cairns, Australia, telling me many stories about the bush. Some of these stories taught me about certain foods called bush tucker. Others taught me about the places I should stay away from because of the dangers there. Still other stories were similar to *Pheasant and Kingfisher*, teaching me how things came to be.

Arone Raymond Meeks

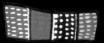

Long, long ago, two men came from far
in the north-west, from the other side
of Bathurst and Melville Islands.
One was called Bookbook, the
Pheasant. The other was Bered-bered,
the Kingfisher.

Both of them carried firesticks and
as they came along they set fire to the
dry grass. Each night they made camp
and each morning they started off
again. They walked on and on, with
their palm-leaf baskets of fresh water
to drink when the country was dry.

It was a long way to travel. But at
last they came to the place they
wanted, where bamboo spears grew
beside the stream.

They heard the bamboo stems
whistling together, and the
mosquitoes were thick down by the
water, so they camped a little way off
on higher ground.

They stayed there for a long time.
One day they would go hunting and
bring back plenty of food, and the
next day they would just stay in their
camp. Often they would sing and
dance together; and they were busy
cutting bamboo spears with sharp
points, and carving spears with strong
wooden blades.

At last they had a visitor, a man
called Nadjalambau.

"I left a lot of men back that way,"
he told them. "They are coming to kill
you. This place belongs to them, and
you should have asked them first
before you cut all those bamboos.
What are you going to do?"

They talked together for a while,
and the two men gave him food and
meat before he went home.

Then Bookbook and Bered-bered
began to get ready. They were both
clever men and had plenty of power,
and they knew just what to do.

Bookbook painted himself all over
with dark red clay, and a little bit of
white. Bered-bered painted himself
yellow. They made their spears
straight and sharp, and then sat there
waiting.

Soon, as they watched, they saw a crowd of armed men coming up to them. They stood up and began to throw their spears. But spears were flying all over the camp. There were so many men, all throwing spears, that Bookbook and Bered-bered couldn't dodge them. They grew weak and short of breath.

"Let's get away now," they said to each other. It was time for them to use their power.

Feathers were starting to come out all over their bodies, and their arms were turning into wings.

Bookbook put bamboo spears and his spear thrower at his back, and they grew into a wide, fan-shaped tail. Bered- bered made his tail from a burning firestick.

Their enemies were trying hard to spear them, but now it was too late. The two men flew away from them, high into the sky. They did not talk like men any more.

"Bookbookbookbook!" Bookbook was a pheasant now.

"Bered-bered-bered!" His friend was a kingfisher.

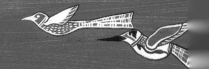

As they flew, their enemies on the ground below them turned into stone. You can see them there today. But the two men turned into birds; and they still fly about, calling out their own names.

*P*heasant and Kingfisher is one of hundreds of Aboriginal stories recorded by anthropologist Catherine Berndt while working in the north of Australia. She recorded them to learn how Aboriginal people think about their world. She wrote the stories in the local language, Gunwinggu, and then carefully translated them into English.

Some Aboriginal people have said, "The land owns us; we don't own the land." They feel they are part of the land, and from the time they are children they learn the songs and stories about it. For thousands of years, these songs and stories have been part of the people's oral tradition and belief system.

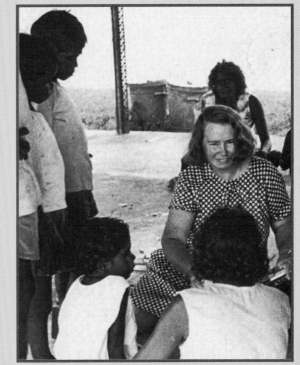

Catherine Berndt collecting stories

Aboriginal artist Arone Raymond Meeks tells us about how he illustrated *Pheasant and Kingfisher*.

"When Catherine Berndt approached me about illustrating *Pheasant and Kingfisher,* I asked myself what I could show of my culture through this story. I decided to fill the art with the symbols and images of Aboriginal people.

I drew the river in the shape of a serpent writhing through the landscape. The serpent, or Rainbow Snake, is found in many Aboriginal stories.

The coolomon, shown with Pheasant and

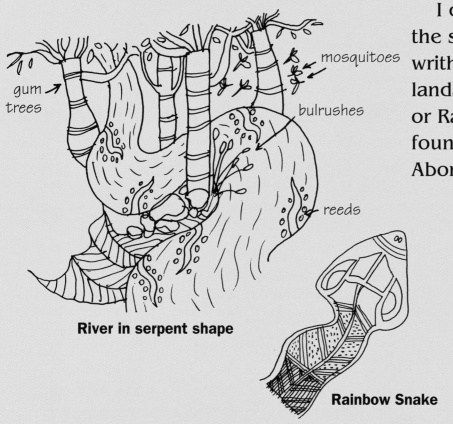

gum trees

mosquitoes

bulrushes

reeds

River in serpent shape

Rainbow Snake

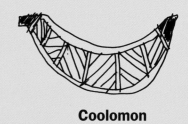

Coolomon

Spear with barbs

Woomera

Kingfisher as they travel, is a carved wood container used by Aboriginal people for gathering food. The spear with barbs and the woomera, or spear thrower, are used for hunting.

In some Aboriginal art, animals are drawn with lines that show how they are cut up for eating. Barramundi, a fish, as well as kangaroo and tortoise are a few of the traditional foods Aboriginal people eat.

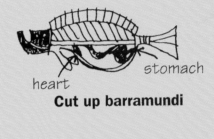

heart   stomach
Cut up barramundi

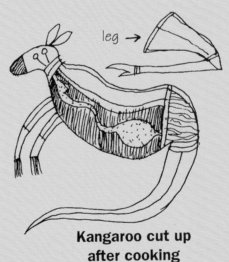

leg →

Kangaroo cut up after cooking

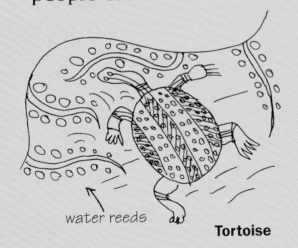

water reeds
Tortoise

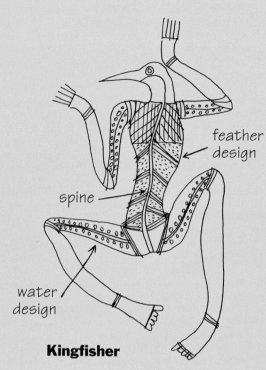

feather design

spine

water design

Kingfisher

For Kingfisher I created feather designs on his body and a water design on his arms and legs. Pheasant, who has a shorter beak, also has the water design on his arms and legs.

Kingfisher dancing

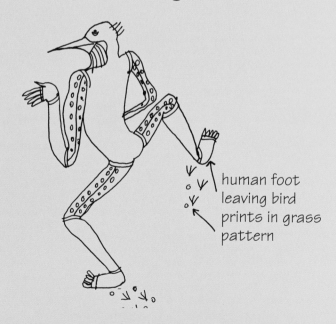

human foot leaving bird prints in grass pattern

I painted the pictures for *Pheasant and Kingfisher* using colors collected from the earth—red ochre, yellow ochre, white pipe clay, and charcoal. These colors are traditionally blended with orchid bulbs to produce a sticky liquid which adheres to tree bark or bodies.

At the end of the story I showed how the men Pheasant and Kingfisher were fighting changed into rocks. This is one way the rocky landscape was created in Aboriginal stories."

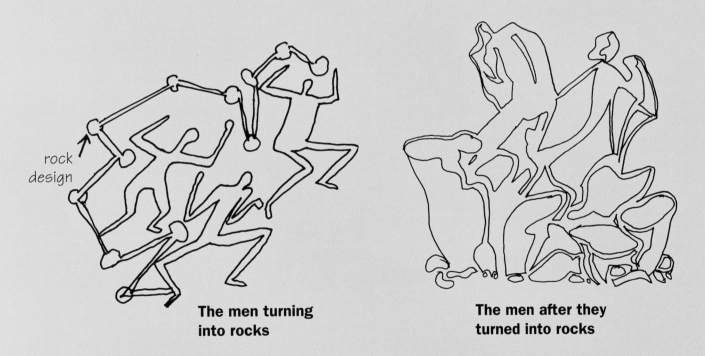

rock design

The men turning into rocks

The men after they turned into rocks